Pirate Name:

_____

_____

_____

The Pirate Who Lost His Name

An original concept by author Lou Treleaven

© Lou Treleaven

Illustrated by Genie Espinosa

MAVERICK ARTS PUBLISHING LTD
Studio 3A, City Business Centre, 6 Brighton Road, Horsham,
West Sussex, RH13 5BB, +44 (0)1403 256941
© Maverick Arts Publishing Limited
Published May 2019

A CIP catalogue record for this book
is available at the British Library.

ISBN 978-1-84886-407-8

Maverick
publishing
www.maverickbooks.co.uk

The PIRATE WHO LOST His NAME

Written by
Lou Treleaven

Illustrated by
Genie Espinosa

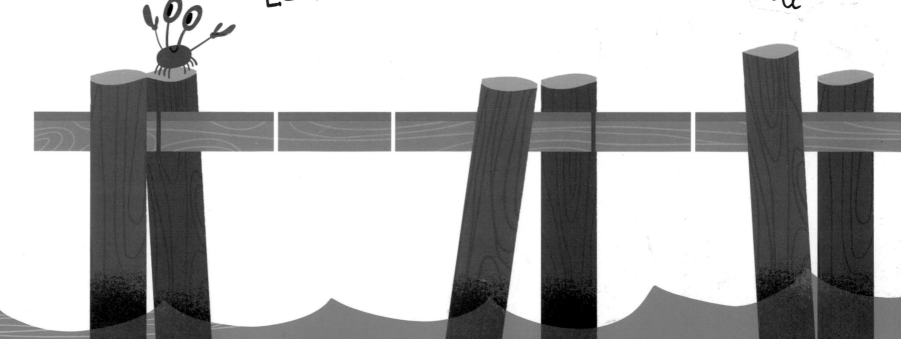

There was once a pirate. A very piratey pirate.
He had everything a pirate was supposed to have.

A curvy sword. A feathered friend. A wooden limb.

He even had a catchphrase.

Yo ho ho and a bottle of orange squash. And a dish of seeds for me parrot.

The only thing he didn't have was a name.

He'd forgotten it.

All his friends had names. There were the boastful pirates:

 Captain Champion

 Captain Wins-at-everything

 Captain My-hook's-bigger-than-your-hook

Then there were the bearded pirates:

Captain Megabeard  Captain Weirdybeard

and Captain There's-parrots-in-me-beard.

Finally, there were the romantic pirates:

Captain Sunset

Captain Stillwater

and Captain Dreamboat.

"Aa-haargh, I wish I could remember me name!"
sighed the pirate with no name.

"Squawk!"
said the parrot.

He was much too embarrassed to ask his pirate friends.
"I know!" he said. "We'll go on a quest. A quest to find me name."
"Squawk!" said the parrot.

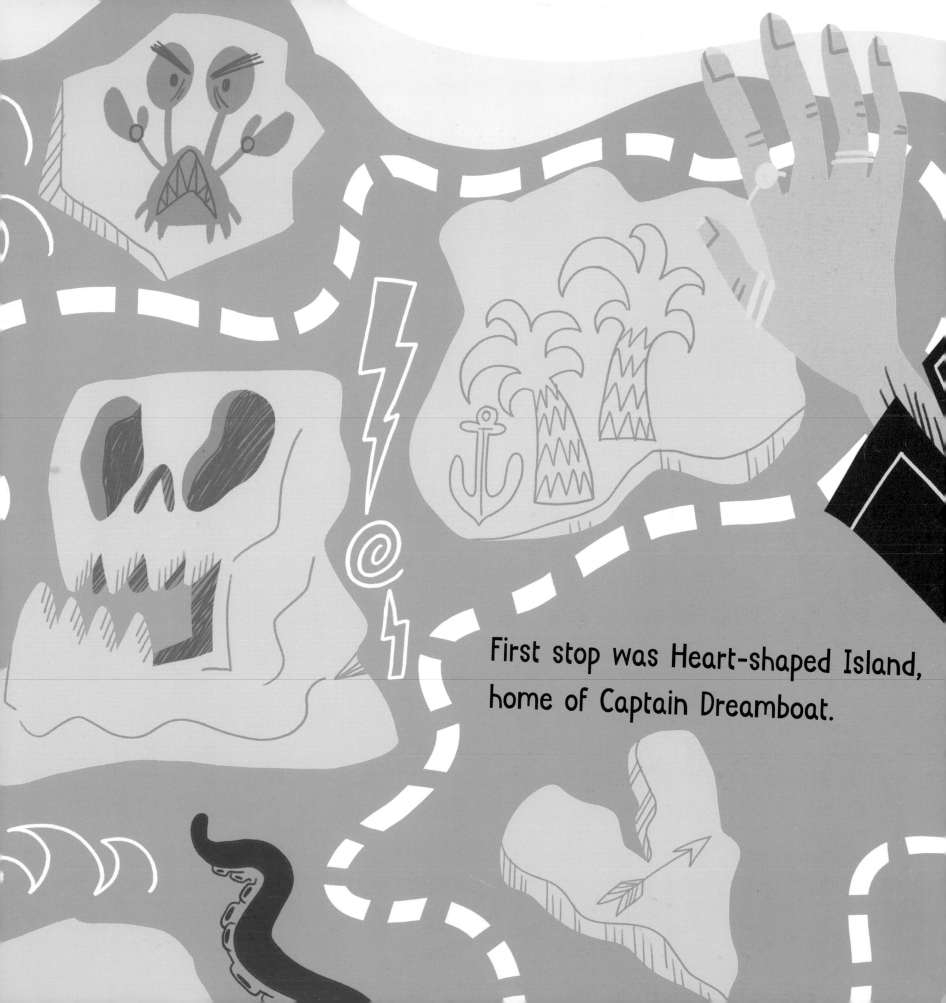

First stop was Heart-shaped Island,
home of Captain Dreamboat.

"Aa-haargh, Captain Dreamboat. Do you still have that birthday card I gave ye?" asked the pirate with no name, hoping he could read his writing on the inside.

"Did it have a picture of me on it? No? Then no,"
said Captain Dreamboat, looking lovingly into a mirror.

Next stop was Captain Anorak's cottage in Collector's Cove. "Aa-haargh, Captain Anorak. Can I have a look at that postcard I sent ye?" asked the pirate with no name, hoping to spot his signature on the back.

"I stuck it into me One Thousand Favourite Pirate Postcards Scrapbook!" said Captain Anorak. "With extra strong glue. Shall we look at 'em together?"

"Er – maybe later," said the pirate with no name, leaving hastily.

"Where to next? I know!"
said the pirate with no name.

"Last year I won the Best Pirate Beard Contest. Me name and picture will be on display at Pirate Lop-It-Off's Barber Shop. We'll go there."

"Aa-haargh, Pirate Lop-It-Off. Where's me picture then?" asked the pirate with no name.

"Sorry," said Pirate Lop-It-Off. "I put up the new winner's picture yesterday."

"Let me guess," said the pirate with no name.
"Captain Weirdybeard? Captain There's-parrots-in-me-beard?"

This year's winner:
Captain There's-a-shark-in-me-beard

"Nearly. It were Captain There's-a-shark-in-me-beard."
"Fair enough," said the pirate with no name.

"I'm never going to remember me name, am I?"
sighed the pirate with no name.

"Squawk!" said the parrot.

"SQUAWK! SQUAWK! SQUAWK!"

"You win. Let's get you some bird seed on the way home, shall we?"

They dropped anchor at Pirate Duff's Bird Stuff.

"There's yer bird seed, me hearties," said Pirate Duff.

"Oh, and ye left yer Pirate Membership Card here last time.

There ye go."

The Very Piratey Pirate
Membership Card

Extra large unlosable version

The pirate with no name looked at his Pirate Membership Card.

"Of course! Me name's **Captain Squawk**. I should have known."
"**Squawk!**" said the parrot.

Name:
Captain Squawk

Pirate ID:
280519

"But if I'm Squawk... who are you?!"

The End